Dear Parent:
Your child's love of reading starts here!

Every child learns to read in a different way and at his or her own speed. You can help your young reader improve and become more confident by encouraging his or her own interests and abilities. You can also guide your child's spiritual development by reading stories with biblical values and Bible stories, like I Can Read! books published by Zonderkidz. From books your child reads with you to the first books he or she reads alone, there are I Can Read! books for every stage of reading:

SHARED READING
Basic language, word repetition, and whimsical illustrations, ideal for sharing with your emergent reader.

BEGINNING READING
Short sentences, familiar words, and simple concepts for children eager to read on their own.

READING WITH HELP
Engaging stories, longer sentences, and language play for developing readers.

READING ALONE
Complex plots, challenging vocabulary, and high-interest topics for the independent reader.

ADVANCED READING
Short paragraphs, chapters, and exciting themes for the perfect bridge to chapter books.

I Can Read! books have introduced children to the joy of reading since 1957. Featuring award-winning authors and illustrators and a fabulous cast of beloved characters, I Can Read! books set the standard for beginning readers.

A lifetime of discovery begins with the magical words **"I Can Read!"**

Visit www.icanread.com for information on enriching your child's reading experience.
Visit www.zonderkidz.com for more Zonderkidz I Can Read! titles.

For you created the deepest parts of my being.
You put me together inside my mother's body.
—Psalm 139:13

Snug as a Bug
Copyright © 2001, 2008 by Amy Imbody
Illustrations copyright © 2001 by Mike Gordon

Requests for information should be addressed to:
Zonderkidz, Grand Rapids, Michigan 49530

Library of Congress Cataloging-in-Publication Data

Imbody, Amy.
    Snug as a bug / story by Amy E. Imbody ; pictures by Mike Gordon.
      p. cm. -- (I can read! Level 1)
    Summary: A mother offers her child many places to sleep, but the child wants
to stay in bed, sleeping as God intended.
    ISBN-13: 978-0-310-71575-7 (softcover)
    ISBN-10: 0-310-71575-X (softcover)
    [1. Beds--Fiction. 2. Animals--Habits and behavior--Fiction. 3. Bedtime--Fiction.
    4. Stories in rhyme.] I. Gordon, Mike, ill. II. Title.
    PZ8.3.I495Snu 2008
    [E]--dc22
                                        2007023108

Art Direction: Jody Langley
Cover Design: Sarah Molegraaf

Printed in China

---

09 10 • 5 4

 ZONDERkidz

Snug as a Bug

story by Amy Imbody
pictures by Mike Gordon

"Would you like to sleep,"

asked Mom,

"like a snug little snail

curled up in a garden pail?"

"No thanks, Mom,

because I can tell

I wouldn't sleep there

very well."

"Then would you like

to sleep in a cave?

That's where the bears sleep!

Are you feeling brave?"

"No thanks, Mom.

I am feeling brave.

But I don't want to sleep

inside a bear's cave."

"Well, now, let me think," said Mom.

"You could sleep like a shark.

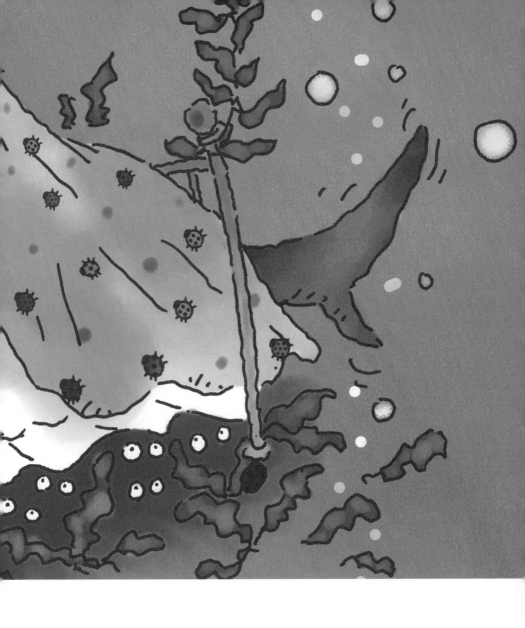

I know that you are not
afraid of the dark.

"Down under the water,

just you and the fish.

You could swim in your dreams

as long as you wish.

"If you don't like that,

then you could try

to sleep upside down,

just like a fly.

"Or sleep like a frog

under mud by the lake,

or under dry logs in the woods

like a snake."

"Dear Mother," said Sam,

"I know this seems wild.

But really,

I just want to sleep like a child."

"Sleep like a child?

Here in your bed?

How did you get

such a thing in your head?

"But if that's what you want,

then close your eyes.

We will pray to God who is wise

and thank him for making you …

"Not a snail,

not a bear,

not a shark,

not a frog,

"Not a fish,

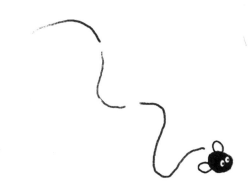

not a fly,

not a snake

on a log.

"But tucked in your bed
with a kiss and a hug,

God's own little child,

as snug as a bug.

"Good night! Sleep tight!"